The Get Rich Quick Club

Also by Dan Gutman

Dan Gutman

The Get Rich Quick Club

SCHOLASTIC INC.

New York Toronto London Auckland Sydney
Mexico City New Delhi Hong Kong Buenos Aires

ISBN 0-439-80156-7

Copyright © 2004 by Dan Gutman. All rights reserved.
Published by Scholastic Inc., 557 Broadway, New York, NY 10012,
by arrangement with HarperCollins Publishers.
SCHOLASTIC and associated logos are trademarks and/or registered
trademarks of Scholastic Inc.

12 11 10 9 8 7 6 5 4 3 2   5 6 7 8 9 10/0

Printed in the U.S.A.   40

First Scholastic printing, October 2005

Typography by Nicole de las Heras

**Dedicated to kids
everywhere
who don't like to read**

Contents

OUR MISSION STATEMENT

We, the members of the Get Rich Quick Club, in order to form a more perfect summer, vow that we will figure out a way to make a

$ MILLION DOLLARS $

by September. We agree that neither rain nor snow nor gloom of night will prevent us from achieving our stated goal, until death do us part. You tried the rest. Now try the best.

Signed,

Ms. Gina Tumolo, 11, CEO

Mr. Rob Hunnicutt, 11, Vice President

Ms. Quincy Biddle, 10, Creative Director

Mr. Edward A. Bogle, 8, Chief Drone #1

Mr. Theodore P. Bogle, 8, Chief Drone #2

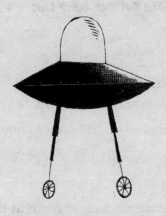

Introduction

It was a dream. I *think* it was a dream, anyway.

I'm just lying out there in the backyard one night, staring up at the sky. Then suddenly a dollar bill lands on my face. I pick it up. It looks real. I have no idea where it came from.

Then another one falls. And another. I look up and see bills fluttering down from the clouds above me. First they come in flurries, and then it turns into a snowstorm of money.

Tens. Twenties. Fifties. Hundreds. They're raining down on me, and *only* on me. It's more money than I could ever imagine. I am incredibly rich. I can buy anything in the world.

The money is piling up high. I grab handfuls of bills and throw them into the air for the fun of it. There's a foot of accumulation on the ground now. I take a running jump into it, like I'm jumping into a pile of October leaves.

Then a blinding flash of white light illuminates the sky. It's so bright, I have to close my eyes. But I can still see the light through my eyelids. It hurts. I scream.

"Gina! Gina!" It's my mother's voice. "Gina, are you okay?"

I open my eyes. I'm in my bedroom now. No light. No money. I get up and rush to the window, half expecting to see the backyard covered in bills.

But there's nothing there. I guess it was just a dream.

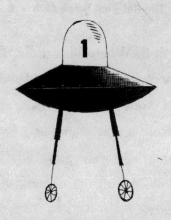

Nothing to Be Ashamed Of

I, Gina Tumolo, love money. So I guess it makes sense for me to dream about it.

I, Gina Tumolo, want to be a millionaire.

There, I said it. I know it's not cool to say it, but it's the truth, so I might as well admit it.

Ever since I was a little girl, I have loved money. In fact, the first memory I have is of money. I was sitting on the couch watching TV one day, and I found a dollar bill stuck inside the cushions. I must have been four years old.

I remember looking at those mysterious markings on the bill. The pyramid with that creepy-looking eye floating through it. What did it mean, I wondered? It all seemed very mystical and magical and wonderful.

I realize that money is just pieces of paper and disks of metal. But from a very young age, I was aware that those papers and disks were powerful. They could be exchanged for *other* things. You could turn them into just about *anything*.

This was amazing to me. You could actually walk into a store, hand somebody some green pieces of paper, and then take something from the store to bring home with you. To keep!

Incredible! And the more of that green paper you had, I quickly learned, the more stuff you could bring home.

Wow! What a fantastic idea! I wanted to get as much of that green paper as possible.

I never had many toys when I was little. My parents didn't have much money back then. Whenever I asked for something, they would give me the old line "It costs too much," or "Money doesn't grow on trees." Maybe that's why all I ever wanted was to accumulate as much money as I could.

We learned in school that King Tut became the ruler of all Egypt when he was about my age, eleven. He owned all the treasures of the kingdom. Bill Gates, I know, started Microsoft when he was barely twenty, and it wasn't long before he became the richest person in the world.

Why not me? I asked myself. Why can't I, Gina Tumolo, accumulate a vast fortune at a very young age? What's stopping me?

Nothing. Other kids want to be in the Olympics, or they want to become rock stars or presidents. Good for them. I want to be a millionaire. My goal is to make my first million before I'm a teenager.

This is the story of the most amazing summer I ever had. It was the summer I started the Get Rich Quick Club.

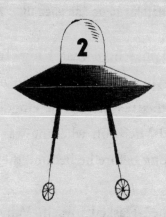

A Simple Solution

I live in Farmington, Maine, which is about thirty miles from Augusta. That's the state capital.

It was dreary the day after school let out for the summer. I was bored and lonely. There's a field out back behind our housing development with one big tree in it. I was walking around, trying to think of something to do with my summer, when I spotted something in the tree.

I went to get a better look. As I got closer, I realized the thing in the tree was Rob Hunnicutt. He lives a couple of houses over and goes to my school. Rob was in the other fifth-grade class.

Rob was sitting up in the tree, and sitting next to him was his pet pig, Chester. Not many kids own a pig, but Rob is a little . . . I guess you could say unusual. He has wild blond hair, and I'm not sure he knows what a comb is.

"Whatcha doin'?" I asked.

"Existing," Rob replied. "Chester and I are inhaling air and letting it escape into the atmosphere."

"Why are you doing it in a tree?" I asked.

"Well, I was thinking that one day this tree might get cut down and made into a fence or a cardboard box or somebody's garage. I wanted to enjoy it while it was still alive."

"*Okayyyyyy. . . .*"

Maybe "unusual" isn't the best term to describe Rob. In truth, most kids think he's a bit of a yo-yo. Sometimes when he says things like that, I think he's putting me on, but I know he isn't. Rob just sees the world differently from other people. He's probably a genius.

"Why don't you join us," Rob suggested. "Chester likes company."

I didn't have anything better to do. I found a low branch that I could dig a sneaker into and climbed up on the tree, giving Chester a pat on the top of his head. The pig oinked contentedly.

"Are you going to camp this summer?" I asked Rob.

"My folks don't believe in camps," he replied. I remembered that Rob's parents were real back-to-nature types. "They say planned activity in an artificial environment stifles creativity."

"I wish I was going to camp," I said. "I waited the whole school year for summer to come, and now I have nothing to do. This is going to be the most boring summer ever."

"You know, a person's average life expectancy is less than eighty years," Rob informed me. "That's eighty summers of living. We've already used up eleven. More than one-eighth of our lives."

I had never looked at it that way. Rob was always thinking of things that made you look at the world in a new way. In this case, it only made me depressed. It reminded me that I would be twelve in a year, and I wasn't even *close* to making my first million.

"G'day, mates!"

The voice came from below. Rob and I immediately knew it was Quincy Biddle. Quincy is a girl who moved here from Australia in the middle of fifth grade. "G'day, mates" is the way Australians say hello.

"Lovely arvo," Quincy said. "Mind if I join the chinwag? I had an appointment at the fang carpenter to adjust my railway tracks."[1]

Australians speak English, but sometimes it's hard to tell. They use a lot of words that don't exactly make sense in America. Like, when Quincy says the phrase "dead horse," she's not talking about a horse that is dead. She means tomato sauce. It was a little weird the first time I went through the lunch line next to her on pizza day.

You know how Eskimos have about fifty different words to say "snow"? Well, Australians have about fifty different ways to say "stupid." If somebody is stupid, you can call them a drongo. Isn't that a great

---

[1] "Nice afternoon. May I join the conversation? I had my braces adjusted by the orthodontist."

word? Or you could call them a boofhead or a ning-nong.

Here are some other words Quincy taught us to use in place of stupid: gumby, nit, alf, mug, deadhead, dipstick, wombat, dill, dag, and ratbag. You'd be surprised how often this comes in handy in everyday conversation.

Rob invited Quincy to join us, and she climbed the tree. Rob, Chester, and I moved over to make room for her.

"Any bities up here?" Quincy asked. "Cripes, I'm stroppy! I just got off the blower with my crumblies. They live out in woop woop, and they must have ear-bashed me for an hour! It seems they got into a bingle and their Toyota is jigged. Now it's not worth a crumpet and they can't flog it. Grandpa's as angry as a frog in a sock!"[2]

Man, I could listen to Quincy talk all day.

---

[2]"Any bugs up here? Good grief, I'm in a bad mood! I just got off the phone with my grandparents. They live out in the middle of nowhere and they must have talked for an hour! It seems they got into an accident and their Toyota is broken. Now it's worthless and they can't sell it. Grandpa's very mad!"

"Blimey!" Quincy exclaimed. "Some ankle biters have lobbed over."[3]

I looked down to see two little kids. It was the Bogle twins, Eddie and Teddy. They're eight, and annoying. Eddie was holding a big wooden box in his hand.

"Whatcha doing in the tree?" Teddy asked.

"Trying to hide from you gerbils," I replied.

"Can we climb up?" they asked simultaneously.

"No!" Rob, Quincy, and I replied. Chester oinked.

They didn't go away. I knew they wouldn't. The Bogle twins never go away. They're like those inflatable punching bags. No matter how many times you knock them down, they always come back for more punishment.

"What's in the box?" I asked Eddie.

"I'll tell you if you let us up."

"It's against the law for second graders to climb trees," Rob informed the twins.

"It is not," Teddy countered. "I climb trees all the time."

---

[3]"Darn! Some little kids have arrived."

"The police haven't caught you yet," I said. "Once they do, they'll throw you in jail."

"I don't *wanna* go to jail!" wailed Eddie.

"Oh, come on up and have a pozzie,"[4] Quincy said, extending her hand to them. Eddie stopped crying immediately, the little faker.

"Okay, we let you up," I said. "So what's in the box?"

Eddie opened the box. It was filled with clumpy dust, like what you'd find if you opened up a vacuum cleaner bag.

"It's from my mommy's clothes dryer," he explained. "She lets me clean the lint screen."

"You collect *dryer dust*?" Quincy asked, unbelieving.

"Sure!" Teddy said. "Soon we'll need a bigger box."

Rob, Quincy, and I looked at one another. These Bogles were weird.

"My grandpa planted this tree, you know," Eddie told us. "He throwed a seed into a hole in the ground right here and planted it himself."

---

[4]"Oh, come on up and have a seat."

"Is that the fair dinkum?"[5] Quincy asked.

Rob and I rolled our eyes. We both knew the Bogle twins were compulsive liars who would make up any kind of nutty story that came to their minds. I had already heard that the Bogles' grandpa was the first man on the moon, the inventor of Silly Putty, and George Washington's photographer.

"Ain't that right, Teddy, about Grandpa planting this tree?"

"Yup. Our grandpa was Johnny Appleseed."

Rob and I snickered. We could have told the twins that the tree wasn't an apple tree. We could have told them Neil Armstrong was the first man on the moon. We could have told them that photography wasn't invented until way after George Washington was dead.

But that would have spoiled the fun. Listening to the Bogle boys tell their tall tales was just about as entertaining as anything on TV, and somehow it helped us forget that we had two months of summer ahead of us with nothing to do.

---

[5] "Is that the truth?"

"You sprogs are a cack,"[6] Quincy chuckled.

"What do you wanna do?" I asked when we had tired of teasing the clueless Bogles.

"I don't know," Rob said. "What do *you* want to do?"

"We could go to the flicks," Quincy said.

"I don't have any money," I muttered.

"Bowling?" Rob suggested.

"That costs money too," I reminded him.

"Why don't we go to the playground?" Teddy Bogle suggested. "Going to the playground doesn't cost anything."

"Going to the playground is no fun," I informed him. "If it was fun, it would cost money. Anything fun costs money."

What a depressing thought. Money was the thing I wanted more than anything, and I didn't have any of it. I had spent my birthday money, and Christmas wasn't for months. This was a serious problem.

"Do you know what makes the world go around?" I asked the group.

---

[6]"You little kids are funny."

"The gravitational pull of the sun?" Rob guessed.

"No," I replied.

"Wind?" guessed Quincy.

"Oink?" oinked Chester the pig.

"A giant hamster?" guessed Teddy. "Running on a treadmill?"

"No," I told them. "It's *money*. Money makes the world go around."

They all looked at me.

"Money can't buy world peace," Rob said.

I turned to him. "Who needs world peace when you can buy a piece of the world?"

"I've got a piggy bank at home," Eddie Bogle announced.

"How much money do you have in it?" I asked.

"None," he replied. "All I have is the piggy bank."

I *told* you Eddie was annoying.

"Come on, blokes," Quincy said. "Hit your kick."[7]

We emptied our pockets. I had a dime. Rob had a nickel, two pennies, and a half a pack of Life Savers.

---

[7]"Come on, you guys. Open up your wallets."

The twins each had a penny that their mother had given them for good luck.

"I haven't a brass razoo,"[8] Quincy said, pulling out what she called a zack, which is some Australian coin that isn't worth much in Australia and isn't worth *anything* here. Together, we didn't even have enough money to buy a pack of gum.

"This is just shrapnel," Quincy moaned, counting up the change. "You can't even buy an icypole with this."[9]

"We need to make some *real* money," I told the group.

"Me and Eddie get ten dollars a month in allowance," Teddy said.

"Allowance?" I laughed. "That's chicken feed! You know what you can buy for ten dollars? A bag of horse manure."

To be honest, I had no idea how much a bag of horse manure cost, but it was the first thing that came to my mind.

---

[8] "I hardly have any money."

[9] "This is just small change. You can't even buy a Popsicle with this."

"Ten dollars for a bag of horse poop?" Quincy marveled.

"Does the horse get to keep any of that?" Rob asked. "It's only fair."

"Why would anyone buy horse manure?" asked Quincy.

"It's used for fertilizer," I explained.

"I thought horse manure was free," Quincy said.

"Free?" Rob twisted up his face as if he smelled it. "Somebody who has a lot of horse manure should *pay* you to take it away."

"That's gross!" exclaimed the Bogle twins.

I was sorry I ever brought up horse manure in the first place.

"My point is," I tried to explain, "ten dollars isn't *real* money."

"So what's real money?" Teddy asked.

"A hundred dollars," I said. "A thousand. A hundred thousand. A million dollars. Lots of zeroes. *That's* real money."

"How are we gonna get that?" Teddy asked.

"We could rob a bank," Eddie suggested.

"Illegal, dangerous, and immoral," Rob responded.

"We could flog some cookies,"[10] said Quincy.

"Nah, too boring."

"We could sell our blood," I said.

"What?" everybody asked.

"You know, sell our blood to a blood bank."

"Who's gonna buy blood?" Teddy asked.

"They use it in hospitals, drongo," Quincy explained, "for transfusions."

"My uncle got transfused," Eddie said. "He had to move to Chicago."

"Your uncle got trans*ferred*, ning-nong," I noted.

"I wonder what costs more," Rob wondered. "Blood or horse manure? It would be pretty incredible if the blood was cheaper."

"I'm not selling *my* blood," Teddy insisted. "I'd die without it."

"You don't flog *all* your blood, boofhead," Quincy said with a laugh. "You just flog a little."

"I'm not flogging *any* of my blood," Teddy insisted,

---

[10]"We could sell some cookies."

wrapping his arms around himself protectively.

"I've got it!" I said, snapping my fingers. "I know a way we can make some real money."

They all looked at me.

"It's simple," I said. "We'll start our own company."

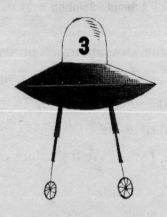

The Get Rich Quick Club

It was so obvious! Why hadn't I thought of it earlier?

Starting your own company was the American way. Anybody who ever got rich did it by starting their own company. So if we started our own company, we could get rich just like all those other rich people. That was the way I figured it.

My mom started her own company a few years ago. It didn't seem so hard.

"Wait a minute," Rob said. "Kids don't start companies."

"Why not?" I replied. "Is there some law that says a group of kids can't start a company?"

"I think it would be grouse,"[1] Quincy said.

"My uncle Donald started a company," Eddie announced. "It's called McDonald's."

"Oh, hush up." I wasn't in the mood to listen to Eddie's stories. The wheels were turning in my head. There were a lot of things that had to be done.

"Yeah, let's start a company," Teddy said.

"Bloody oath!"[2] Quincy agreed.

They all sat there for a few seconds in silence until Rob piped up. "How do you start a company?"

"Well, the first thing you need is a name," I informed them all. "Take Kodak, for instance. Do you know how they got the name Kodak?"

"Doesn't 'Kodak' mean 'camera' in Swedish or something?" Rob asked.

"Nah, 'Kodak' doesn't mean *anything*," I said. "I read about it in a book. The guy who started Kodak liked the letter K. He just made up the word 'Kodak.'"

---

[1] "I think it would be cool."

[2] "Yeah!"

"That must have been a real Kodak moment," Rob said.

"I like the letter W," Eddie told us.

"My favorite letter is X," said Teddy.

"Nobody cares what letters you sprogs like," I snapped.

"Maybe we can make a name out of our names," Rob suggested. "Like the RobGinaQuincy Club."

"Or GinaRobQuincy Club," I said.

"Or QuincyRobGina," said Quincy.

"What about us?" Eddie whined. "We want our names in there too."

"The name is too long already," I told the twins.

"What about initials?" Rob said. "We could call it GRQ, for Gina, Rob, and Quincy."

I thought about that. GRQ. It had a ring to it. Like IBM, or CNN. Then something occurred to me.

"You know," I told the others, "GRQ stands for something else besides Gina, Rob, and Quincy."

"What?" They all looked at me expectantly.

"Get rich quick!" I said.

And that was how we named the Get Rich Quick Club.

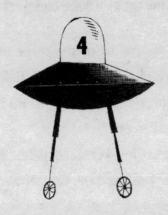

The Fine Points of Business

I could see the future—we'd have a big office building someday with the letters GRQ on it. Secretaries running around. A company jet. Warehouses scattered around the world. Everyone on the planet would know about the Get Rich Quick Club.

"The next order of business is a company motto," I said.

"What's a motto?" Teddy asked.

"I don't know, what's a motto with you?" Rob cracked.

"A motto," I explained, "is a slogan. Like 'All for one and one for all.' That's the motto of the three musketeers."

"I thought the motto of the three musketeers was 'Creamy, chewy, chocolate filling,'" Teddy said.

"Not *those* three musketeers!" I said irritably. "The other three musketeers."

"There were six musketeers?" Eddie asked.

"How about 'You tried the rest. Now try the best'?" Rob suggested.

"That's not bad," I said. "Did you make that up?"

"No," Rob explained. "I saw it on a pizza box."

"The next order of business," I told them, "is that we need to have company bylaws. Bylaws are the rules of the company. You've got to follow the rules. If we don't have rules, everything falls apart, and the next thing you know, we would be like savages, killing each other over a piece of meat."

"What kind of bylaws?" Quincy asked.

"Well, for instance," I said, "we all have to promise that we won't run over each other with our bikes. That would be dangerous, right? So anybody who runs over another member of the GRQ with their bike should be kicked out of the GRQ. See what I mean? Can you think of any other bylaws we should have?"

"How about we can't hit each other over the head with sharp sticks?" Eddie suggested.

"Well, of *course* that one," I agreed. "Hitting each other over the head with sharp sticks can't be allowed."

"How about drowning?" suggested Teddy.

"Okay, okay. No drowning either." I realized that introducing the idea of bylaws might have been a mistake.

"Poisoning?" Eddie asked.

"Throwing each other off cliffs?" Teddy said.

"There aren't any cliffs around here," I said impatiently.

"True enough," Rob said. "But the twins bring up an excellent point. What if we go on a business trip somewhere and they have cliffs there? What if one of us gets upset and pushes another one of us off? What will happen if we don't have any bylaw to cover it?"

"Okay, okay," I agreed. "No throwing each other off cliffs. That's enough bylaws. Let's move on. We have to give out titles."

"Titles?" Quincy asked. "What do you mean, titles?"

"Your job," I explained. "Your position. In a real company, every employee has a title. For starters, I think I should be CEO."

"I wanna be CEO!" Eddie shouted.

"You don't even know what 'CEO' means," I said.

"I don't care," Eddie whined. "It must be something good or you wouldn't want to be it."

"'CEO' stands for chief executive officer," I said. "The boss."

"Well, aren't *you* the ant's pants?"[1] Quincy snickered.

"How come *you* get to be CEO?" Teddy complained.

"Because this whole thing was my idea," I explained calmly. "Rob will be vice president."

"What about me?" Quincy asked.

Quincy was new to our school, but she was already famous for being really artistic. She could draw just about anything on demand, without even having to trace it.

"Quincy will be the creative director," I decreed.

---

[1] "Well, you think you're pretty great, don't you?"

"And the twins, you will be secretaries."

"I don't wanna be a secretary!" Eddie immediately started wailing, as if I had said he would be beaten with a tennis racket.

"Secretaries have to answer the phone," whimpered Teddy.

"Well, you don't have to worry about that," Rob pointed out. "We don't have a phone."

"Then we'll have *nothing* to do!" Eddie whined. "At least if we had a phone, I could answer it."

The rest of us rolled our eyes.

"How about drones?" Rob suggested. "You two can be the company drones."

"What's a drone?" Teddy and Eddie asked suspiciously.

"Drones are very important," Rob told them. "A drone is like a busy bee in a beehive. That means you get to deliver secret messages and stuff. I wish I could be a drone."

"Delivering secret messages sounds cool," Eddie said.

"And remember," I added, "we'll *all* be on the company board of directors."

"Okay, put us down for that drone thing," Eddie agreed. "As long as we are going to be the *chief* drones."

"Chief drones it is," I said. "You'll be drones number one and number two. Every other day you can switch numbers to make it fair."

I wasn't about to tell the Bogle twins that a drone was a male slave to the queen bee in a hive. Sometimes with little kids, the less they know the better.

Now that titles had been given out, I realized I had assembled the perfect team. I would be the heart, soul, and brains of the operation. We would count on Rob's genius to come up with the idea that would make us a million dollars. Quincy, with her artistic ability, would help us tell the world about it. And the Bogle twins, well, they'd do the dirty work and other stuff that the rest of us didn't want to do.

We were ready to take on the world.

"Quincy!" a voice called out.

"Crikey, it's my mum," Quincy complained. "Time

for tucker. I hate to pike out, cobbers. Gotta bail. See you in a divvy. Hoo-roo."[2]

"Wait a minute!" I stopped Quincy from climbing down the tree. "Doesn't she know we're having a company meeting?"

"How would she know?" Rob said. "The company didn't exist ten minutes ago."

"Look," I told Quincy. "Just because your mom's calling doesn't mean you have to leave."

"But she's my oldie!"[3] Quincy said. "Besides, I'm so hungry, I could eat a horse and chase the jockey."

"Don't you know anything about negotiations?" I told her. "When your mom says to come home, it doesn't necessarily mean *now*. That's just her first *offer*. Tell her you'll be home in ten minutes."

"Ten minutes, Mum!" Quincy called fearfully.

"Good," I said. "You gotta be tough to succeed in business."

---

[2]"Oh, no! It's my mother. Time for dinner. I hate to leave early, friends. Gotta go. See you soon. Good-bye."

[3]"But she's my parent!"

"Quincy! I need you home in five minutes!"

"See?" I pointed out. "Your mother didn't need you home *now*. Tell her you'll be home in eight minutes."

"But—"

"Tell her!"

"Eight minutes, Mum!" Quincy yelled.

"Six minutes!" Quincy's mother hollered. "Or we hop into the grub without you!"[4]

"See," I explained to everybody. "You've learned the first lesson in business negotiations. Never grab the first offer they put on the table. Okay, I propose we adjourn this meeting. That means we go home and eat."

"I have a question," Eddie said, raising his hand as if he was in school.

"Yes, drone number one?"

"What is the GRQ Club going to *do*?" Eddie asked. "Doesn't a company have to *do* something or sell something? How are we gonna make money?"

"An excellent question," I told Eddie. "Now I see

---

[4]"Six minutes! Or we start eating without you!"

why we gave you the responsibility of being chief drone. Let's meet back here tomorrow afternoon. Put on your thinking caps. We'll come up with a master plan to make a million dollars."

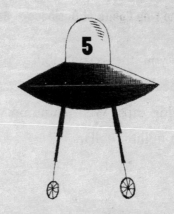

A Million-Dollar Idea

There's an old, weather-beaten gazebo out in the field behind my house. I thought this would make a good office for the GRQ Club. Of course, once we got rich, we would buy a real office building.

I brought along a stapler, some tape, paper clips, pens, a ruler, scissors, and a calculator. An office needs office supplies, right? I had a big metal box with a lock on it to keep all the stuff in. I also brought along a photo of Bill Gates, my hero and inspiration.

"Who's the nerd?" Quincy asked when she saw me taping the photo up to the post.

"Bill Gates," I told her. "He's the richest man in the world."

"Looks like a nerd."

Quincy had made a couple of signs to put up too. The first one was a logo she had designed for the company. It looked like this:

I told Quincy she had done beautiful work. The second sign said:

> ☠ **WARNING: KEEP OUT!** ☠
> **MAN-EATING PIRANHAS INSIDE!**

"Piranhas live in water, gumby," Rob said as he pulled up on his bike. "Not gazebos."

"I know that," Quincy explained. "But this will get them thinking, won't it? Nobody can steal our company secrets."

"We don't have any secrets," Rob said.

"Not yet we don't," I told them. "But soon we will. Good thinking, Quincy."

Finally the Bogle twins showed up, carrying their silly box of dust. I sat everybody down on the benches and stood up to address them.

"I would like to call to order the first official meeting of the GRQ Club," I began. "If any of the members are opposed, let them speak now or forever hold their peace."

Everybody just sat there. The Bogle twins picked their noses.

"When we last met," I continued, "we formed our company. We came up with a company motto. We established bylaws and assigned positions. Someday, when we're all multimillionaires, we'll think back to that lazy day when we started this whole thing. But for now, we need to come up with the way we'll make a million dollars. Does anybody have any ideas?"

Everybody still sat there. The Bogle twins still picked their noses. It didn't look good.

"I gotta pee," Teddy finally announced.

"I know!" Quincy said. "I could design some grouse togs and we could flog them around town!"[1]

"It costs a fortune to manufacture clothing," I told her. "We'd have to set up a factory overseas."

"We could sell our old toys," Teddy suggested.

---

[1] "I could design some cool clothes and we could sell them around town!"

"Nobody wants your old, broken, spit-up-on toys," I said.

"I've got an idea," Rob chimed in. "Let's put an ad in the paper asking a million people to each send us a dollar. Then we'll have a million dollars. We don't have to make anything or sell anything."

"That's berko!"[2] Quincy exclaimed.

"Okay, how about this idea," Rob continued. "You know those little packs of ketchup they give out in fast-food restaurants?"

"Yeah . . ."

"You know how squishy they are?"

"Yeah . . ."

"I always liked squooshing them with my fingers. I could do it for hours."

"Your point?" I demanded.

"I was thinking," Rob said, "they should make pillows out of those things. You know, big ones for people to sleep on. We could start a company making ketchup-filled pillows. You could even microwave

---

[2]"That's crazy!"

them so they'd be warm when you went to bed."

Rob *is* a genius, but I didn't want to be the one to tell him that was a dumb idea.

"You've gone round the bend, haven't you?" Quincy asked Rob. "Microwaved pillows? Have you got kangaroos loose in the top paddock?"[3]

"It was just an idea," Rob added sheepishly. "I never said it was a *good* idea."

"I gotta pee," Teddy reminded us.

"You should have thought of that before the meeting," I told him.

"How about we write a rap song!" Eddie suggested. "Rappers make millions of dollars."

With that, Eddie began to improvise a little rap song, and did a little dance as he sang it:

> *"I hate everybody, yes I do.*
> *I hate you and you and you.*
> *I hate your father and I hate your mother,*
> *I hate your sister and I hate your brother.*

---

[3]"You've gone crazy, haven't you? Microwaved pillows? Are you dumb?"

I'd put you in the zoo, and then I'd say boo.

I'd throw you in a freezer till you're an old geezer.

I could throw you off a cliff, and then you'd be stiff.

I'd dump you in a truck—"

"Zip up, sprog!"[4] Quincy said.

It was obvious that we weren't going to make a million dollars with any of these dumb ideas. There was a great idea out there somewhere, but we just hadn't found it yet. I was getting frustrated.

"I'm up a gum tree,"[5] Quincy said, sighing.

"We could wash cars, I suppose," Rob suggested. "Or sell lemonade."

"Wash cars?" I muttered disgustedly. "Sell lemonade? Are you joking? The key word in the Get Rich Quick Club is *quick*. You think you're going to get rich quick selling lemonade for a quarter a cup? You think

---

[4]"Shut up, you little brat!"

[5]"I don't know what to do."

you're going to get rich quick washing cars? You might as well wait around for a UFO to land in your back-yard."

When I said those words, Rob suddenly got this amazing look in his eyes.

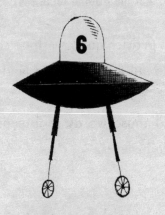

Big Bikkies

Say that again!" Rob said excitedly.

So I said it again: "You think you're going to get rich quick washing cars? You might as well wait around for a UFO to land in your backyard."

"That's *it*!"

Rob bounced up off the bench like he had springs in his feet. He paced back and forth as the idea formulated itself in his head. We all watched him. You could almost hear the synapses in his brain firing like machine guns.

He had a wild, excited look in his eye. It was the same look that you see in the eyes of mad scientists and lunatics in movies when they are planning to take over the world. If this had been a cartoon, a giant light bulb would have been floating over his head. I had the feeling that he was going to come out with something totally brilliant.

"*What's* it?" I asked.

"I just figured out how we can make a million dollars," Rob announced enthusiastically. "It's simple, it's easy, and it's quick."

"What? What? What?" we all begged.

"We'll have a UFO land in our backyard!"

What a letdown! Here I thought Rob was going to come up with some brilliant plan, and he comes up with something as stupid as his microwave pillow idea. My heart sank.

"I hate to break it to you," I told Rob, "but there *are* no UFOs. Even if there were UFOs, it's not like you can just tell them where to land."

"I know there are no *real* UFOs," Rob said, still with a mischievous smile on his face. "But what if we made our *own* UFO?"

"Oh, choof off, Rob." Quincy smirked. "You're a fruitcake."[1]

"I'm listening," I said, trying to keep an open mind.

"Don't you see?" Rob said excitedly. "We'll make our *own* UFO, and take pictures of it!"

I thought about that for a few seconds. Then I realized he was *right*! Rob had a can't-miss, slam-dunk, cash-the-check, million-dollar idea.

"You . . . are . . . a . . . genius," I told him.

"It's nothing, really."

"No, I mean it, Rob," I said. "Your brain has connections the normal brain lacks. You make Albert Einstein look like the dumb kid at school. This is the greatest idea since the invention of the wheel!"

The twins were still looking like they didn't get it. So I laid it out for them.

"We'll make our own UFO and shoot pictures of it. Then we'll sell the pictures to all those cheesy newspapers they sell at the checkout line at the supermarket. We'll shoot video of the UFO and sell it to sleazy

---

[1] "Oh, get out of here, Rob. You're crazy."

TV shows. They love that stuff. Soon companies will be all over us offering to make UFO posters, UFO lunch boxes, UFO toys, UFO trading cards, UFO backpacks—"

"Don't forget UFO T-shirts," Rob added.

By then, the others had finally caught on to the plan and saw the potential. We were all on our feet now, jumping up and down with excitement, clapping Rob on the back.

"I know exactly how to shoot the photo," Quincy bubbled. "We're gonna make big bikkies!"[2]

"We're gonna be millionaires!" I said, just loving the sound of the word in my mouth.

"Billionaires," said Eddie.

"*Trillionaires!*" said Teddy.

We were so excited that we kept on jumping up and down, and we didn't stop jumping up and down until the Bogle twins said they had to go to the bathroom.

---

[2]"We're gonna make lots of money."

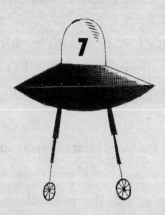

7

Undoubtedly Fake Flying Objects

The next morning, we all gathered excitedly at the gazebo. Quincy arrived carrying armfuls of junk. Frisbees. Frying pans. Aluminum pie plates. Garbage can covers. Old toys. Round pillows. A fishing pole. Some other junk. Around her neck was a Polaroid camera she had borrowed from her parents. Quincy was the artistic one of the group, so I put her in charge of the photo shoot.

"I brought the UFOs!" she said as she attached an aluminum pie plate to the fishing line with some tape. She had Rob hold out the fishing pole so that the pie plate dangled in the air. Quincy got down on her knees so she could point the camera upward at the pie plate. She explained that the photo would look most real if there were trees and sky in the background. She took a few shots of the pie plate hanging from the fishing pole, and we gathered around her to look at the pictures as they developed.

Well, it didn't look like a real UFO at all. The fishing line was visible. In fact, the fishing *pole* was visible at the top of the photo. Instead of a UFO, it looked like an aluminum pie plate dangling from a fishing pole. We were all disappointed, except for Quincy.

"Cool bananas,"[1] she said. "Forget the fishing pole idea. We've just gotta chuck things up in the air and shoot them."

"Hey," Rob suggested, "let's chuck the Bogles' box of dust up in the air."

The Bogles started crying, of course, until Rob assured them he wouldn't do it.

Quincy told Rob to pick up a garbage can cover and

---

[1]"Everything's fine."

fling it as high as he could, like a Frisbee. She got the camera ready.

"Okay, give it a bash!"[2] she said.

Rob heaved the garbage can cover up into the air and Quincy took the shot.

"Oh, pig's bum!"[3] she moaned. "Missed it."

I told the Bogles to retrieve the garbage can cover. Rob tossed it up again. This time Quincy said she got it right in the middle of the viewfinder. We all gathered around to look at the picture.

"Let me have a squiz,"[4] Quincy said, holding the photo close to her face.

"What's it look like?" asked Eddie, who was too short to see.

"It looks like somebody threw a garbage can cover up in the air," Rob said. He was right. That was exactly what it looked like. The picture wasn't going to fool anybody.

---

[2]"Okay, give it a try!"

[3]"Oh, that's not right!"

[4]"Let me have a look."

"No worries," Quincy said cheerfully. "We've got to fuzz it up a bit. You know, so you're not sure what it is. She'll be apples."[5]

Quincy's camera had a dial on it that let her change the shutter speed. She said that if she slowed down the speed of the camera's shutter as it opened to expose the film to light, a moving object would be a little bit blurry in the picture. I didn't know much about photography, but it sounded like it made sense.

We tried it again a bunch of times, with Rob heaving stuff up in the air. Quincy fired away with the camera, trying to catch the "UFO" as it flew by.

I kept looking around, hoping that no other people would come by. It might be embarrassing to be seen throwing pots, pans, pillows, and other strange objects up in the air to photograph them.

The pictures were looking a little bit more like UFOs, but they weren't perfect. They still looked a little fake. Quincy wasn't discouraged. She told us that in real photo shoots, photographers will sometimes

---

[5]"Everything is fine."

take hundreds of pictures before they get one they like.

"Let's give these bodgy snaps the flick," Quincy said, tossing the stack of photos aside. "They're not worth a crumpet."[6]

The camera was out of film. Quincy opened another film pack and loaded it. The rest of us gathered more stuff that might resemble a UFO.

"Okay," Quincy said as Rob got ready to toss an old plastic toy up in the air. "Give that thingamajigger a burl."[7]

They made the shot and again we all gathered around to see the result.

"Well," Quincy said, not all that enthusiastically, "it's better than a poke in the eye with a blunt stick."[8]

"It's pathetic," I complained. I was getting impatient. I was beginning to think this UFO thing might not have been such a good idea after all. "These aren't UFOs,

---

[6]"Let's throw those crummy pictures away. They're worthless."

[7]"Okay, try that thing."

[8]"Well, it's better than nothing."

they're UFFOs. Undoubtedly fake flying objects."

"Don't get niggly,"[9] Quincy said. "We're getting there."

She shot some more photos. Some of them were pretty good, but they still looked phony to me. By this time, the Bogle twins' attention span was just about used up. Instead of helping us with the photo, they were now running around playing tag with each other.

"Maybe we should call it quits," Rob told Quincy. "We could save the rest of the film and try again tomorrow."

"Nah, you might as well just blow the film," I instructed her. "Tomorrow we'll just have to come up with another million-dollar idea."

"I have only one shot left anyway," Quincy told us.

"Let's make it count," Rob said. He got one of Quincy's round pillows and threw it up in the sky.

While the pillow was in the air, Eddie and Teddy were chasing each other around, not looking where they were running. They didn't see Quincy as they got

---

[9]"Don't get irritated."

close to her, and Quincy didn't see them because she was looking into the viewfinder. I was the only one who could tell there was going to be a collision.

"Watch out!" I yelled.

It was too late. Eddie Bogle slammed into Quincy just as she pushed the button on the camera. He knocked her to the ground.

"Cripes! You little germs!" Quincy shouted. I had never seen her so angry. "Can't you jacks-in-the-box behave? Pull your socks up! You ruined it, you dumb wallies!"[10]

"I didn't mean to!" Eddie whined. He put his hands over his face in shame.

"Oh, man, that was our last shot!" Rob said disgust-edly.

We all helped Quincy get up off the ground. Rob picked up the camera. It seemed to be okay. The pic-ture Quincy had taken was lying in the dirt. She picked it up and was about to toss it on the pile of

---

[10]"Darn! You little obnoxious brats! Can't you crazy kids behave? Get your act together! You ruined it, you idiots!"

rejects, but the image was beginning to come up, so she watched it.

"Hang on a tick,"[11] she said, some excitement building in her voice.

The rest of us gathered around for a peek. As the picture developed, we could see that it didn't look like any of the other photos Quincy had taken. The impact of Eddie smashing into her just as she snapped the picture had shaken the camera. The picture was fuzzy, but not so fuzzy that you couldn't make it out. There it was—a lifelike UFO hovering over the trees.

"Well, I'll be stuffed!" Quincy exclaimed. "It's a ripper!"[12]

---

[11]"Wait a second."

[12]"What do you know? It's great!"

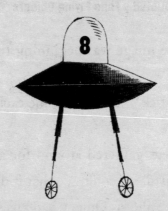

The *National Truth*

The five of us gathered around looking at our photo, like football players in a huddle.

"It's perfect," Rob announced. "Just perfect."

"It's dinkie-di," Quincy said. "This snap is crash hot."[1]

"I gotta pee," Teddy said.

"There's only one way that anybody would be able to tell this photo is a fake," I told the others. "And that's if one of us spilled the beans."

"What do beans have to do with it?" asked Eddie.

"It's an expression, dingbat," I told Eddie. "It means

---

[1] "It's for real. This picture is wonderful."

to reveal a secret."

So together we made a pact. A solemn vow. The five of us agreed that we would tell everybody we had been out in the field playing when this UFO buzzed by. It stopped over the trees, hovered there for a second or two, and then it zipped away. We just happened to have a camera with us and were lucky enough to snap this fuzzy picture.

That was the story, and we all promised to stick with it. We agreed that if any one of us revealed that we had faked the photo, terrible, horrible things would happen to that kid. I thought it would be a good idea to seal our vow with blood. Nobody wanted to bleed, so we used grape juice instead.

That afternoon, we all rode our bikes over to the supermarket. They've got a rack of newspapers by the cash register that aren't really newspapers. They look like newspapers, but the stories don't sound anything like the stories you read in regular newspapers. WOMAN GROWS PUMPKIN IN THE SHAPE OF THE PRESIDENT'S HEAD! JFK LIVES . . . IN THE WHITE HOUSE BASEMENT! MY TWIN BROTHER IS FROM MARS! That sort of thing.

All of them looked like the kind of newspaper that might go for a story about UFOs. We decided to buy one called the *National Truth*. The cover headline read:

METEOR ON COURSE TO DESTROY EARTH NEXT WEDNESDAY.

We dug into our pockets and came up with $2.40. "Will we get this back?" asked Rob.

"Listen," I said. "It's our capital. Think big. Think of it as an investment."

"Oh, great," said Rob. "We don't get it back."

"Can we at least get some gum with it?" asked Teddy.

The $2.40 in investments was enough to buy the *National Truth*, with exactly enough left over for a pack of Bubblicious gum.

On the way back, we split up the gum. Once we got to the gazebo, we found the page in the *National Truth* where they had the mailing address. Rob worked out a letter to include with our photo:

Dear National Truth,
We are five children who live in
Maine. We created this fake UFO

photo and we thought you might be able to use it in your paper. Please get back to us as soon as possible.

Sincerely,
The Get Rich Quick Club

"Are you crazy?" I asked Rob after I had read his letter. "Do you honestly think they're going to go for that?"

"Well, it's the truth," he replied.

"The truth is boring," I told him. "Nobody's gonna pay us a million dollars for the truth."

Lying, I realized, just didn't come naturally to Rob. Even though he was the genius in our group, it would be up to me to compose the letter. So I did:

Dear National Truth,

I am a 55-year-old man with a wife, children, and no history of mental problems. The other day I was in the field behind my house when I saw a weirdly shaped object in the sky. I happened to have my camera with me and snapped the enclosed photo. I thought you might like to use it in the National Truth. The price for this photo is one million dollars. I would appreciate it if you would pay in cash. Please get back to me as soon as possible.

Sincerely,
Herb Dunn

"Who's Herb Dunn?" Eddie asked.

"How should I know?" I replied. "I made him up."

Carefully, we slipped the letter and photo into an envelope. Quincy put the address of the *National Truth* on the outside and enough stamps to send two ounces. (She even weighed it on a little scale she found in her father's study.) She wrote UFO PHOTOS, DO NOT BEND on the envelope, too. We sealed it up and walked it over to the mailbox at the end of the block. All five of us crossed our fingers for good luck as we dropped it into the slot.

"All we can do now," I said, "is wait."

So we waited. And waited. And waited some more. It seemed like it took forever.

While we were waiting to hear from the *National Truth*, I worked up a profit and loss statement and presented it to the rest of the company at our next meeting.

"It doesn't look like we're doing very well, does it?" Rob noted.

"Every company takes a while to turn a profit," I said. "We just have to be patient."

PROFIT AND LOSS STATEMENT	
EXPENSES	
Film (pay back Quincy)..	$10.95
National Truth..	1.75
Bubblicious gum..	.65
Postage (pay back Quincy's dad)............................	.60
	$13.95
INCOME	
None..	0
NET LOSS	$13.95

"But it's already been two whole days!" Eddie moaned. Eight-year-olds are not exactly good at delaying gratification.

"Do you know how long it took Walt Disney to build his company?" I asked the group.

"No . . ."

"Neither do I," I snapped. "But believe me, he didn't do it in two days."

Finally, everybody got tired of waiting to hear from the *National Truth* about our photo. They started bugging me to call them on the phone and see what was taking so long. I held the kids off for a week and then agreed to make the call.

The phone number inside the *National Truth* got me into a confusing voice-mail system. I had to punch a bunch of numbers, but finally I got one of the editors on the phone.

"Eve Stropper," she said gruffly. "What is it?"

"I'm calling from Maine," I told her. "I sent you a genuine UFO photo. Did you receive it?"

"Which UFO photo?" she said, unimpressed. "We

get hundreds of UFO photos."

I described the photo and the envelope it was in. Eve Stropper put me on hold while she looked around her office.

"Oh yeah, got it right here," she finally said. "But something tells me your name isn't Herb Dunn."

Oops! I had forgotten I'd written the cover letter saying I was a fifty-five-year-old man.

"I . . . uh . . . well . . ."

"It doesn't matter, kid," Eve Stropper said. "You did a nice job on this picture."

"What do you mean?" I asked.

"Who's kidding who, kid? This picture is as phony as a three-dollar bill."

"How can you tell?"

"Because *all* UFO photos are phonies." She laughed.

My heart sank. Quincy, Rob, and the Bogle twins were looking at me, trying to figure out what was going on. "How much are they going to pay us?" Rob whispered.

"Then you won't print it?" I said into the phone.

"I didn't say that," Eve Stropper replied. "Kid, we print phony UFO pictures all the time. The only problem is we just ran a big UFO piece a couple of weeks ago. Didn't you see it? It was a story about aliens taking over the Earth by hiding secret messages in McDonald's Happy Meal toys. You see, there's a secret code on the bottom of each toy. When three-year-olds see the code, they go insane."

"But three-year-olds can't even read yet!" I told her.

"Who cares?" Eve Stropper said. "It was our best-selling issue since the one with exclusive photos of Laura Bush sneezing."

"That was news?" I asked, amazed.

"She had never been photographed in mid sneeze before," she replied. "Anyway, we can't run another UFO piece for a while. Try me again in about a year."

"A year!" I exclaimed. "That's like forever."

"Sorry, kid," Eve Stropper said. "If we ran UFO photos every week, they'd have no shock value. We'd lose our credibility. Readers would start to believe the pictures were faked."

"But your pictures *are* faked!"

"Well, we don't want *them* to know that," Eve Stropper said with a chuckle. "Hey kid, you sound like you're pretty bright. Did you shoot any pictures of Elvis Presley or Marilyn Monroe lately?"

"Didn't they die a long time ago?" I asked.

"So what?" she said. "They still sell papers. To their millions of fans, they live forever."

"No," I said. "I don't have any photos like that."

"Too bad. We haven't run a good Elvis sighting in a long time."

I asked her to send the photo back to us and hung up the phone. The *National Truth* was *not* going to pay us a dime, much less a million dollars.

The Big Payoff

When I told everybody that the *National Truth* wasn't going to use our photo, they all acted like it was the end of the world. They were moping around, hanging their heads, all depressed. As CEO of the company, it was part of my job to keep up the company morale.

"Are you going to let one little failure knock you down?" I said, pacing around the gazebo. "What do you think GRQ stands for? The Gang of Real Quitters?"

"Maybe shooting fake UFO pictures wasn't such a good idea after all," Rob grumped. "It was dishonest. It was cheating. It was—"

"It was brilliant," I interrupted. "Do you think Bill Gates gave up the first time somebody told him no?"

"Did Bill Gates try to flog fake UFO snaps too?" Quincy asked.

"That's not the point," I told her. "The point is that we're not quitters. If at first you don't succeed, try, try again, right?"

"Try *what* again?" Teddy asked.

"Try another paper," I told him. "If the *National Truth* doesn't want our photo, somebody else will."

The Bogle twins would pretty much go along with anything I told them to do, but Rob and Quincy were not all that enthusiastic about sending the photo to another paper and waiting weeks to hear back. They argued that the other sleazy papers like the *National Truth* probably had boxes full of UFO photos that readers had sent in. They were probably right.

The *Farmington Journal* is our local paper. It's skinnier than most other newspapers and only comes out once a week. In the *Farmington Journal*, it's a big news story when a school crossing guard retires. That's front-page news. The rest of the paper is filled with announcements, like what day people should put their cans and bottles out in front of their houses for recycling. Stuff like that.

We figured the *Farmington Journal* might be interested in our photo. After all, as far as we knew, there had never been a UFO sighting in Farmington, Maine. Rob made me promise not to pretend to be somebody else when I called the offices of the *Journal*.

"*Journal*," a man's voice said.

"May I speak with one of the editors, please?" I asked.

"You're talkin' to *all* the editors. Brian McNight. I'm the editor, and the owner, and I sweep up around here too. What can I do for you?"

"Mr. McNight, my name is Gina Tumolo," I said, trying to sound as serious as possible. "I am an eleven-year-old girl, and my friends and I spotted a UFO recently."

"Kid, I'm busy," Mr. McNight said.

"Don't hang up!" I shouted into the phone. "We have a photo of the UFO."

"Oh yeah?" he said, a little interest in his voice.

"You kids shot a picture of a UFO right here in Farmington?"

"That's right, and we were thinking that maybe you might want to put the picture in the *Journal*."

"What does this so-called UFO look like?" he asked.

"It's . . . sort of hard to describe," I stammered. What was I going to say? It looks like a round pillow we threw up in the air? "You'd have to see it."

"I have a hole to fill in next week's issue," Mr. McNight said. "Why don't you bring your photo over so I can take a look at it? It might make a good human-interest story."

Well, Rob, Quincy, and the Bogles were about as excited as puppies at dinnertime. They wanted to go over to the *Journal* right away, until I reminded them that we didn't have the photo back from the *National Truth* yet.

When the photo did arrive two days later, we rode over to the *Farmington Journal* office like we were Olympic bicycle racers. Panting and out of breath, we left our bikes in a pile and dashed inside. The receptionist asked us who we were, and we told her we had come to see Mr. McNight. She called him on the intercom and led us down the hall to his office.

Brian McNight was a heavy man with a mustache. His desk was cluttered with papers, coffee cups, Chinese-food containers, and junk.

"Don't tell me, let me guess," he said when we burst into his office. "You're the kids who saw the UFO, right?"

"How did you know?" Rob asked.

"I've got ESP. I'm on deadline. Lemme see your photo."

I handed him the UFO picture, and he looked it over carefully. Then he took a magnifying glass out of his desk drawer and looked at it even more carefully. He kept stealing glances at us, and we kept stealing glances at one another.

"You shot this yourselves?" he finally asked. "It's not bad. Not bad at all. Now tell me the truth. Is it real?"

I figured Rob—Mister Always-Tell-the-Truth— might crack. It looked like he was about to say something, but I stepped on his foot and he kept his mouth shut.

"Sure it's real!" Teddy Bogle piped up. "I oughta know, 'cause I was the one who snapped it!"

I could always count on the Bogle boys to tell a lie. For once, I was glad I had decided to let them hang around with us.

"Well, this is your lucky day," Brian McNight said. "I was holding page one for the school board election, but they postponed it."

"Does that mean you're going to print our picture?" I asked, trying to pretend I wasn't excited.

"If I don't, I've got a hole on page one the size of Greenland."

"All right!"

We all started jumping up and down and yelling like game show contestants who had won the grand prize.

"Calm down," Mr. McNight said. "This isn't a playground."

I gathered my composure and went back to Mr. McNight's desk. It was time to "talk turkey." That's what my dad always says when it's time to discuss money.

"How much will you pay us for the photo?" I asked.

"Well, how much were you expecting?" he replied.

"We were thinking," I said bravely, "of a million dollars."

"I'm thinking of a million dollars too," he said, smiling, "but I'll pay you fifteen."

"Fifteen *million*?" Rob said, gasping. I thought his eyeballs were going to pop out of his head.

"No."

"Fifteen thousand?" Quincy asked.

"Fifteen," Mr. McNight repeated. "One . . . five. That's a ten-dollar bill and five singles. I think you kids are old enough to do the math."

Fifteen dollars! He had to be kidding. Mr. McNight pulled a ten-dollar bill and five singles out of a box on his desk, holding it out to me. I wasn't about to accept his first offer.

"We're willing to negotiate," I said. "How about a *half* a million dollars?"

"Fifteen bucks," McNight replied. "Take it or leave it."

"Will you excuse us for a moment?" I asked, pulling the others out into the hallway.

"Sure."

"What do you think?" I asked the group.

"We could flog it to another rag," Quincy suggested.

"They might say the same thing," I said.

"Maybe we should take the money," Rob suggested. "Fifteen bucks is fifteen bucks. That's more than we have now."

"Kids," Mr. McNight shouted from his office, "I don't have all day."

"Okay," I shouted back. "We'll take the fifteen dollars."

When I went back to his office, Mr. McNight handed me the money and also a yellow piece of paper.

"Sign this," he said.

"What is it?"

"A contract," he said. "It basically says we paid you the fifteen dollars, and the *Journal* owns the rights to publish the photo."

The contract was only one page, but the page had a lot of words on it. They were printed in really small letters. I couldn't even figure out what half the words meant. But I didn't want to look stupid. I nodded my head knowingly and signed the line at the bottom of the paper. I handed the sheet to the others for them to sign.

"Great, kids," Mr. McNight said as he walked us back to the reception area. "Look for your photo in next week's *Journal*. If you want, you can stop by the office and I'll give you some extra copies to put up on your refrigerators at home."

We rode our bikes home from the *Journal* a lot slower than we rode them getting there. Personally, I felt guilty. After teaching the others the fine art of negotiation, I had negotiated a crummy deal.

"I think we got the rough end of the pineapple,"[1] Quincy muttered as we pedaled.

"He took advantage of us because we're kids," Rob commented.

"You can't even buy a video game with fifteen dollars!" Eddie Bogle complained.

---

[1] "I think we got a bad deal."

"Hey, we made fifteen bucks," I said, trying to look on the bright side. "That's better than nothing."

"We sold our souls," Rob said dejectedly as we pulled into the gazebo, "for fifteen lousy dollars."

"Don't think that way," I told him. "Sure we sold our souls. But this is just the beginning. You'll see. We're going to make millions from this. So down the road we will have sold our souls for a million dollars. Does that make you feel any better?"

"No," Rob said.

I put the fifteen dollars into our metal box, and everybody went home without saying good-bye.

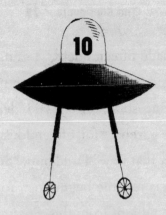

Alert the Media

While we were waiting for the *Journal* to publish our UFO picture, I made up another profit and loss statement and presented it to the group.

PROFIT AND LOSS STATEMENT

EXPENSES

Film (pay back Quincy)...	$10.95
National Truth...	1.75
Bubblicious gum...	.65
Postage (pay back Quincy's dad)............................	.60
	$13.95

INCOME

Sale of photo..	$15.00
NET PROFIT...	$ 1.05

Pretty pathetic. Summer was nearly half over, and all we had earned was $1.05. We could have made more money selling lemonade.

But then, in next Thursday's mail, there it was—the *Farmington Journal*. Splashed across the front page was our photo and a big headline:

UFO SIGHTED IN FARMINGTON?

This is what the caption under the photo read:

This alleged UFO was photographed by eight-year-old Theodore Bogle of Farmington last week, when he was play-ing in the field by the Franklin County Fairgrounds with his brother Eddie and friends Rob Hunnicutt, Quincy Biddle, and Gina Tumolo.

For the moment, I wasn't thinking about how we had been ripped off by the *Journal*. I was thinking about how cool it was. That was *our* photo, right in the newspaper! I grabbed for the phone to call Rob.

"Did you see it?" he hollered as soon as he heard my voice. He sounded just as excited as I was.

"Doesn't it look cool?"

We arranged to get the Get Rich Quick Club together at the gazebo to celebrate.

"What's all the fuss?" Mom asked as I was hanging up the phone. Then I showed her the paper.

"You saw an alien spaceship," she asked, astonished, "and you didn't tell me?"

"I . . . forgot."

"You *forgot*?" Mom put her hand over her heart like she was going to faint. "You spotted an alien spacecraft and you *forgot*?"

This is a lesson that every kid should learn as early in life as possible. Pay attention now. If you ever get caught in a lie, don't admit it. Don't deny it. Just say, "I forgot."

You see, forgetting stuff is not quite as bad as lying, and nobody can ever prove you're lying when you say "I forgot." Believe me, this is bulletproof. I pull this off all the time, and it never fails.

"Yeah, I forgot," I told her. "Is forgetting against the law?"

Mom started giving me the usual lecture about telling the truth or doing the right thing or some other such mumbo jumbo, but I was already out the door.

By the time I got to the gazebo, Quincy, Rob, and the Bogle twins were already there. They were looking over their own copies of the *Farmington Journal* excitedly.

"I can't believe they actually put our UFO photo in the paper!" Eddie Bogle marveled.

"Boy, did we put a swiftie over on them!"[1] Quincy beamed.

While we were buzzing, a white van pulled up to the street closest to where we were sitting. It had one of those satellite dishes on the roof and CHANNEL 6 NEWS painted on the side. A bunch of people piled out with cameras and other equipment. They started lugging it over to the gazebo.

"Are you the kids who spotted the UFO?" a blond

---

[1] "Boy, did we fool them!"

lady asked, sticking a microphone in my face.

"Uh . . . yeah," I said. I figured that as CEO, I should be the spokesperson for the group.

"Where did you see this UFO?"

Two big video cameras were trained on me. I felt like I was an animal in the zoo. I glanced at Rob for help, but he clearly didn't want to do the talking.

"It was over there somewhere," I said, pointing in the general direction of the field where we had shot the picture.

"What did it look like?"

"I . . . forget," I stammered. Almost immediately, I realized that "I forget" works much better with parents than it does with the news media.

"You forget?" the lady asked. I didn't want to look at her, because it's easier to lie to somebody if you're not making eye contact with them. The only problem is, not making eye contact with somebody is a sure sign that you are lying. So either way you lose. That's another one of those life lessons that every kid should learn as soon as possible.

"Well, it was sort of nondescript looking," I explained.

"Yeah, it didn't have a specific look about it," Rob said, trying to bail me out.

"It was sort of . . . general looking really," I added lamely.

We all stood around shuffling our feet for a while until Eddie piped up.

"It was *humongous*!" he exclaimed, spreading his arms as wide as they would go.

The cameramen turned away from me like I had bad breath, and he stuck the cameras in Eddie's face. He didn't seem to mind at all.

"And it had big glowing green lights!" Eddie continued.

"Yeah!" agreed Teddy. "And it made a weird humming sound!"

Rob, Quincy, and I waved our hands at Eddie and Teddy, trying to shush them, but it was no use. Once you got those twins started telling stories, there was no way to stop them. And the camera crew was lapping it up like starving animals.

"A weird humming sound?" the reporter asked. "Can you describe it for us?"

Eddie and Teddy pinched their nostrils together and started humming. The noise they produced sounded like one of those annoying Hawaiian hula songs. The reporter turned to me again.

"Is that what it sounded like to *you*?" she asked.

"Uh, yeah, something like that."

Well, what was I going to do, tell the *truth*? If I admitted that we had faked the UFO picture, our whole story would be blown. This was our chance to get famous and make some money. I just wished those Bogles would keep their mouths shut. If they exaggerated too much, our story would be blown anyway.

"And then," Eddie said, almost in a whisper, "the spaceship landed in the field over there and the aliens came out!"

Oh no.

I looked at Teddy with murder in my eyes, but he wasn't paying attention. He was busily concocting the next part of the ridiculous story in his head, I was sure.

"You actually *saw* the aliens?" The reporter was down on one knee now, so she could get on the same level as Eddie and Teddy. A cameraman elbowed me out of the way so he could get a better shot of the twins. I don't know why people always think twins are so adorable.

"Sure!" they exclaimed simultaneously.

"We saw the aliens! They even *talked* to us!" said Teddy.

Rob, Quincy, and I rolled our eyes. I knew what they were thinking. Those little Bogle twerps were ruining *everything*. We should have put muzzles on those sprogs to shut them up. How come for once in their lives they didn't have to go to the bathroom?

"What did the aliens say to you?" the reporter asked breathlessly.

Eddie looked at Teddy. Teddy looked at Eddie. Rob looked at Quincy. I just cringed. Who knew what crazy thing the Bogles might come out with?

"'Inky dinky pinky,'" Eddie said.

Oh man. If he had said something like "Take me to

your leader," it would have been almost believable. But "inky dinky pinky"? Nobody would buy that in a million years!

"'Inky dinky pinky'?" repeated the reporter. "The aliens said, 'Inky dinky pinky'?"

"Yeah," Teddy agreed. "Just like that they said it. 'Inky . . . dinky . . . pinky.'"

"Is that true?" the reporter asked me, Quincy, and Rob. We looked at one another.

"Well," I finally said. "The sound was muffled and difficult to understand, but it sounded something along the lines of 'inky dinky pinky.'"

"This is fascinating!" exclaimed the reporter. "What do you think 'inky dinky pinky' means? Could it be some . . . secret code?"

"It must be some sort of high-level communication system that humans don't have the intelligence to understand," Rob guessed. "Or maybe it's an intergalactic nursery rhyme." Even Rob was getting into the spirit of lying!

"Was that *all* the aliens said?"

"Yup," Teddy replied. "Inky dinky pinky. Then they

got back inside the UFO and it flew away."

Before the newspeople had gathered up all their equipment, the Bogle twins managed to tell them that the aliens were twelve feet tall, hairy all over, and had noses on the back of their heads. Rob, Quincy, and I made no effort to stop them. It was no use. The newspeople even seemed interested in the stupid box of dust the Bogles carried with them everywhere.

Afterward, Teddy and Eddie were strutting around as if they had just won the lottery.

"We're gonna be on TV!" they chanted. "We're gonna be on TV!"

"Why did you make up all that stuff?" I scolded them. "You made us look like a bunch of idiots! They're never going to use that video. You ruined everything!"

"We were only trying to help," Eddie whined. I thought he and Teddy were going to start crying, but they just hung their heads.

It was really all my fault, I realized. As head of the company, I never should have let the twins get into a position where they could mess things up. As soon as the TV crew arrived, I should have asked Rob or Quincy to get the twins out of sight so they couldn't say anything stupid. They weren't old or mature enough.

Certainly they weren't old enough to lie convincingly. Only when a kid reaches the age of ten or eleven can he tell a lie good enough for grown-ups to believe. I should have known that. How stupid of me!

All our hard work shooting the fake UFO pictures was for nothing. I was crushed and defeated. Now we would have to come up with *another* plan to make a million dollars.

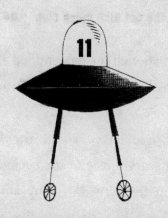

Fame and Fortune

Well, I guess I overestimated the intelligence of the human race. I assumed that when the Bogle boys started spinning their ridiculous tale of our "alien encounter," Channel 6 would kill the story and show some *real* news. But I was wrong. Not only did they put us on TV, but they even ran us as the top story on the news that very night.

There I was, watching TV, and suddenly our gazebo appeared on the screen.

"This is Channel 6 News," the lady reporter said as she walked through our field. "The quiet village of Farmington was rocked today when it was revealed that five youngsters spotted an unidentified flying object in this field last week and managed to snap a photograph of it."

As Eddie Bogle talked about the UFO landing, Channel 6 put scary music in the background and our UFO photo on the screen. To my amazement, they were treating our UFO "sighting" like it was for *real*.

Well, let me tell you, it took about thirty seconds for word to get around town. For the next few hours, the phone in our house did not stop ringing. Everybody I knew called, plus a lot of people I didn't know. It was the same at Rob's house, Quincy's house, and *especially* at the Bogles' house.

People wanted to know what we saw. What color was the UFO? (No color—there *was* no UFO.) Were we scared? (Of what?) Did we think the aliens might return? (Of course not. They were never here to begin with.) And most of all, people wanted to know what those mysterious words "inky dinky pinky" meant.

I didn't have a lot of answers.

A couple of days after we were on the local TV news, *USA Today* ran an item about us, and that's when the story exploded all over the country.

Suddenly, our little town was the UFO capital of the world. People started streaming into Farmington like gold had been discovered here.

First it was the UFO nuts, as Rob called them. They came from all over, sniffing around for evidence. You could tell who they were right away, because they were all walking around with fancy cameras, looking up in the air, ready to take a picture at a moment's notice. With no UFOs to shoot, they took pictures of the spot where we had seen the UFO.

UFO nuts were camping out in the field, hoping the UFO would return. While they waited, we could see them skulking around the grass with tape measures, metal detectors, magnifying glasses, and binoculars. One guy from California set up a portable satellite dish and told everyone that he was going to capture the next transmission from outer space. Somebody else claimed he'd decoded the words "inky dinky pinky" and declared that it meant "we'll be back."

The media jumped all over our story. UFO "experts" analyzed our photo on TV and argued about whether or not it was real. *Sixty Minutes* devoted a show to UFOs ("The Myth That Will Not Die").

Before this, I had had no idea that UFO sightings drive some people into a frenzy.

A lot of other people came to town just because it seemed like the place to be. Families would drive into downtown Farmington on Saturday on the off chance that they might see a UFO. They would end up spending a lot of money in the local stores, and the mayor proposed putting up a big billboard on the highway to draw in more tourists. Somebody suggested changing the name of Farmington to UFOville.

Up to this time, Farmington's only claim to fame was that Chester Greenwood, the guy who invented earmuffs, used to live here a long time ago. But this was something completely different. It was the most exciting thing to happen in Farmington since some flood washed away just about the whole downtown sixty years ago. You could feel the excitement in the air. All anybody talked about was the UFO sighting.

Meanwhile, me and Rob and Quincy and the Bogles were becoming celebrities. Every day another reporter would be asking for an interview. A camera crew came all the way from Japan to talk with us. We got so many phone calls that the twins' parents had to get an unlisted number. People would stop us on the street to take our picture.

After the UFO article ran, the *Farmington Journal* had to print ten times as many papers as usual, so they kept running follow-up stories about us. They interviewed our teachers, our friends, anybody who ever knew any of us.

Photographers hid in the trees outside our houses with lenses as long as my arm, waiting to shoot pictures of us. Reporters would follow us down the street shouting out questions: "Are you hiding aliens?" "Were the aliens friendly?" And, of course, "Is the picture real?"

The Bogle twins were the most popular of all. People would come up to them asking for autographs. Eddie and Teddy could barely write in cursive, but people wanted them to sign autographs! Some kids in Missouri started a Bogle Brothers Fan Club. At least three websites devoted to the Bogles popped up. They put a photo of their stupid dust box online.

You'd go by the Bogles' house, and there would be reporters and photographers hanging around, waiting for the twins to come out. There was an item in the paper about some Hollywood producer who wanted to tell the Bogle twins' life story.

It was ridiculous! It seemed that a couple of years before, they weren't even toilet trained, and now people wanted to see their life story!

The only people who didn't fall for our hoax were the kids we knew from school. They all knew right away that we had faked the UFO photo, and they thought it was a big hoot that the rest of the world didn't catch on. I suppose that's why none of them told on us.

"This is Captain Moonbeam from the planet NiCAd," some kid said when I picked up the phone one day. "Deliver a pizza to the gazebo at eight o'clock and we will take it with us back to our home planet. Extra cheese." Then he started giggling and hung up.

Much to our amazement, the words "inky dinky pinky" quickly become a national catchphrase.

Everybody started saying it. When Jay Leno or David Letterman told a joke that bombed, they would simply add "inky dinky pinky" at the end, and everybody would crack up.

The newspaper reported that scientists were analyzing the mysterious phrase on computers to determine what the hidden meaning was. It wasn't long before we started seeing T-shirts that said INKY DINKY PINKY on them.

That got me a little angry. This was *our* hoax. If anybody should be making money off it, it should be *us*. That was why we shot the fake UFO pictures in the first place.

There was no need to worry about money, though. Pretty soon the offers started pouring in. A company that made disposable cameras wanted us to be in their commercial, acting out our UFO sighting. Somebody who made breakfast cereals wanted to put our picture on the box of a new UFO cereal that had little marshmallow flying saucers in it. My dad, who is a lawyer, said he would help us handle all the paperwork as soon as these companies put their offers in writing.

We got offers from companies that wanted to make alien wind-up toys, inflatable unidentified flying mobiles, unidentified flying tub blocks, unidentified flying candy in flying saucer–shaped containers. Even the *National Truth*, which hadn't wanted to publish our photo in the beginning, was leaving messages on my home answering machine. Now they were offering thousands of dollars just to talk to us. Sweet!

"Big bikkies!" Quincy bubbled. "We're gonna make big bikkies!"[1]

A million dollars started to sound like small change. We were going to be more successful than I ever imagined in my wildest dreams. Once the contracts arrived for all the offers we were receiving, the money would start rolling in by the bucketful.

I had to admit I'd been wrong about those Bogle boys. They had done the right thing by making up that crazy story for the TV cameras. None of this would have happened if not for their wacky imaginations and their skill at lying.

---

[1] "We're going to make lots of money!"

There were some UFO nuts hanging around our gazebo, so Rob, Quincy, the Bogles, and I climbed up into the tree where it had all started for us.

"You know," I said, feeling as good about everything as I could possibly feel, "someday this tree will have a plaque on it in honor of us."

"At my last checkup, the dentist said my teeth had plaque on them," Eddie said.

"It's not the same kind of plaque, dingbat."

Everything was going just as I had hoped. The Get Rich Quick Club was actually going to get rich, quick.

Good Liars, Bad Liars

The next day we held a board of directors meeting up in the tree, where the UFO nuts wouldn't notice us. I had carefully tallied up all the money we would earn if all the offers we had received came through. The total was . . . Are you ready for this?

Ten million dollars.

Quincy just about fell out of the tree when I said that. I was on a high, and I didn't think I'd ever come down. I would be making more money at the age of eleven than most people make in their entire *lives*. When Bill Gates was my age, he hadn't made his first dime yet!

Back in the old days (that is, before we were famous), we used to sit around fantasizing about what we would do if we had a million dollars. Now we were planning what we would actually do with the millions of dollars that would be coming to us.

"I'm going to buy a seven-fifty-seven jet," Quincy said.

"Why?" we all asked.

"So I can go visit my rellies in Australia whenever I want,"[1] she told us. I couldn't argue with that.

"I'm gonna buy the best skateboard in the world," announced Teddy.

"The best skateboard in the world only costs a few hundred dollars, ning-nong," I informed him.

"Oh, then maybe I'll get *two* of them."

"I'm gonna buy the Super Bowl," Eddie said.

"You can't buy the Super Bowl!" Quincy pointed out.

"Why not?" whined Eddie. "I'll have lots of money."

"But the Super Bowl is not a thing you can *buy*," I explained patiently. "You can't buy *everything*. You can't

---

[1] "So I can go visit my relatives in Australia whenever I want."

buy a cloud or an ocean. These things are not for sale. You can't buy Mexico. Do you see what I'm trying to say?"

"Maybe Teddy and I could *chip in together* and buy the World Series," Eddie said.

It was useless.

Rob had been unusually quiet. I asked him what he was going to buy with his share of the money.

"You can't buy happiness," Rob said quietly. "I think I'll give my money to charity."

"Charity?" we all asked, openmouthed.

"There are a lot of poor people who need it more than I do," Rob explained.

I was going to give Rob a hard time about donating his money to charity. But I decided not to. The whole fake UFO idea had come out of his brilliant-but-twisted brain. It figured that he would want to do something weird with the money. He had that right.

"Well, I'll tell you what *I'm* going to do with *my* cut," I announced. "I'm going to invest my money in our company. We need to hire employees now. Rent office space. Print stationery. Set up a line of credit. Hire accountants and lawyers. We need to do all the things a young company needs to do if it wants to grow."

"What?!" Nobody could believe it.

"Do you think Bill Gates took his first million dollars and used it to buy a skateboard?" I scoffed. "No, he put it back into his company. That's why he's the richest man in the world today."

They all said I was crazy, but I didn't care. What did any of *them* know about running a business anyway?

"I'm gonna buy a truck filled with Kit Kats," Eddie suddenly announced.

"No, a truckful of Twix," Teddy said.

Naturally, that led to a heated argument over whether Kit Kats were better than Twix. Personally, I always felt that the caramel in Twix is a distraction from the flavor of the chocolate. If you want the taste of caramel, in my view, you should just buy a caramel. Quincy disagreed, insisting that Kit Kats, without the caramel, were no more than glorified Nestlé's Crunch bars. Rob, strange as he is, said he preferred Milk Duds.

"Milk Duds is a stupid name for candy," I told the group.

"Not as stupid as Mr. Goodbar," Quincy said.

"No, Mr. Goodbar is the perfect name," I told her. "It's a bar, and it tastes good. Compare that with Milk Duds. They're made with milk, which kids are forced to drink, and they're *duds*. Who wants to eat a *dud*?"

"I do," insisted Rob.

We could have argued the point for hours, but some kid ran over to the tree. He was waving a newspaper.

"Did you hear the news?" he shouted.

"What news?"

Wordlessly, the kid handed me the new issue of the *Farmington Journal*. There was a big headline on the front page:

UFO PHOTO WAS FAKED! SIGHTING WAS ALL A HOAX

On the front page was a big article explaining exactly how we had planned and shot our bogus UFO. The paper apologized to the readers for deceiving them.

I felt my heart start beating like there was a bass drum inside me. This couldn't be happening. Not now. Not after all we had been through.

"How did they find out?" I sputtered.

"Beats me," Eddie said, scratching his head.

"Beats you, huh?" I said, pointing a finger at him. "How could you? You blew it for all of us. Do you think any of those companies are going to pay us a *dime* when they find out that we faked the photo? They're going to laugh in our faces. You cost us millions!"

"Don't chuck a spaz, Gina," Quincy said. "No worries."[2]

"We didn't tell!" Eddie and Teddy whined.

"Oh sure!" I was furious now. "We made a pact, remember? We agreed not to tell anybody. We said we would all stick to the story. We promised not to break the oath or terrible, horrible things would

[2]"Don't get angry, Gina. Everything's fine."

happen to us. We sealed it with blood, remember?"

"It was grape juice." Teddy was covering his head like he was afraid that I might hit him.

"That's not the point," I told him. "We made an agreement. I never should have let you sprogs into the company."

"We didn't tell anybody," Eddie said, wrapping his arm around his brother. "Honest!"

"Oh sure, like we can believe anything *you* say!" I fumed. "Both of you are liars!"

"Gina," Rob said quietly, "this time they're telling the truth."

"Huh?"

"The twins didn't tell the newspaper we faked the photos," Rob admitted. "It was me."

"What?! *You?!*"

It was inconceivable to me that Rob would rat us out. He was the most trustworthy kid I ever met.

"*You* told them we faked the photo?"

"I felt guilty," Rob said quietly. "Ever since I came up with the idea of shooting the UFO, I felt guilty about it. I couldn't sleep at night, thinking about it. I guess I'm just not a good liar. It didn't feel right."

"It didn't feel right?" I exploded. "Ten million bucks would have felt right, wouldn't it? Does it feel right to ruin everything for the rest of us? How could you do that? If you had to go and be all honest and moral about it, couldn't you have waited awhile? Couldn't you have waited until after we signed the contracts and collected the money?"

Rob didn't say a word. He just jumped out of the tree and went home.

The End of the Get Rich Quick Club

As I expected, all the companies that were going to pay us millions of dollars bailed out of the deals as soon as they heard the news that our UFO photo was a phony. All the reporters and camera crews and UFO nuts who had invaded Farmington cleared out of town like it was radioactive. Nobody wanted to interview us anymore.

We had already bragged to all the kids we knew, telling them what we were going to do with the money we were going to make, so they made fun of us pretty badly. We were the laughingstock of Farmington.

For days, I couldn't bring myself to speak to Rob. I was so angry at him for leaking the news that I was afraid I might hit him or throw something at him.

But as August passed and I started to think about school again, I saw Rob at the supermarket. For a moment, I thought about ducking out of there before he could see me, but I decided that would be cowardly.

"Look, I'm sorry I yelled and everything," I told him. "I was a jerk."

"I'm sorry too, Gina," Rob said. "I should have thought about you guys before doing what I did."

We agreed that we should have one last meeting of the Get Rich Quick Club, so we could officially shut down the company and clear our stuff out of the gazebo. Rob said that he and his mom were going to buy his back-to-school supplies and soccer gear that afternoon, so we agreed to hold the meeting that night. I said I'd pass the word to Quincy and the Bogle twins.

It was a beautiful night. Not a cloud in the sky. Just one big, round moon. While I waited for the others to arrive at the gazebo, I stared up at the stars. The little chill in the air said that fall was coming. Soon the leaves would start turning colors. The days were beginning to get noticeably shorter.

The others were probably thinking I was going to scream and yell about how we had blown millions of dollars, but I had gotten over my anger. Even though we hadn't gotten rich, the Get Rich Quick Club had accomplished a lot.

"We were a great team," I began when everyone had arrived. "Quincy, we couldn't have done it without you. You figured out how to make a UFO photo that would fool the world. We couldn't have done it without Teddy or Eddie either. You were the ones who got us on TV and made us famous."

They beamed up at me like angels. I don't think they ever fully realized exactly what we had done, or what had gone wrong.

"And Rob, well, if it hadn't been for you, we never would have come up with the crazy idea in the first place."

"We couldn't have done it without you either, Gina," Rob replied. "You were the leader. None of this would have come together if we didn't have you as our CEO."

It was true, and I appreciated that he said it.

"Well." I sighed, unlocking the metal box. "I guess we'd better divvy up the company assets."

There were fifteen dollars in the box. We paid back Quincy the $10.95 she had spent for film, plus the sixty cents she owed her dad for postage. That left $3.45. Rob divided that by five on the calculator from the metal box and came up with sixty-nine cents. Luckily, he had a lot of change in his pockets, so we changed some of the dollar bills, and I handed out the right number of coins to everyone. Then I tore up the last profit and loss statement and dropped it into the box.

"Wow!" The twins marveled as they examined the coins. To them, sixty-nine cents was just about as good as a million dollars.

"Well, that's that," I said, gathering up my stapler, Scotch tape, and other office supplies that I had brought from home. I tore my photo of Bill Gates into little pieces.

"I'm knackered, mates," Quincy said. "Gotta go

stack some zzzzs. See you in the soup!"[1]

The moment after she said that, there was a flash of bright light in the sky just above the horizon. I saw it out of the corner of my eye.

"By jingoes! What was *that*?" Quincy asked.

"It must be a plane," I said.

"That was no plane," Rob insisted. "Planes can't fly like that."

"Maybe it was a shooting star," suggested Teddy.

"I don't think so," Rob said.

Then, right behind us, we saw it. It was a shiny metallic object, shaped sort of like an egg, but about the size of an elevator. It hovered over the field for a moment, and then it swooped down until it rested gently on the grass not more than twenty feet from where we were sitting.

---

[1]"I'm tired. Gotta go get some sleep. See you later."

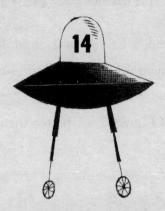

The Secret of the Universe

It was like nothing I had ever seen before. The egglike thing had no lights. We could see it only by the light of the moon. It didn't make any noise. It had come down silently, as if it had cut off its engine and coasted the rest of the way.

"Stone the crows!"[1] Quincy whispered as we stared at the thing. "It's . . . a UFO."

"Everybody stay calm," I said, but I felt my teeth chattering, and the little hairs were standing up on my arms.

---

[1] "Wow!"

"I'm scared," Eddie said, huddling against his brother. "Maybe we should call nine-one-one."

"I gotta pee," Teddy said.

"This UFO looks a lot better than ours did," Rob commented.

"Deadset it does, boofhead,"[2] Quincy told him. "It's *real*."

"You think there's anybody in there?" Teddy wondered. "Or any*thing*?"

"Who knows?" I replied. "Where's the camera?" If we could get a photo of a *real* UFO, it occurred to me, we could make our money all over again and even Rob would feel good about it.

Quincy dug out the camera from a pile of junk. But when she clicked the button, nothing happened.

"The thingamajigger is jigged!"[3] she exclaimed, giving the camera a whack on its side.

"Maybe there's no film in it," Rob guessed.

"Put a new pack of film in!" I barked. "Quick, before the UFO flies away!"

---

[2]"Of course it does, dummy."

[3]"The thing is broken!"

"We don't have any bloody film!" Quincy said in a panic. "Remember, you told me to blow the film shooting the *fake* UFO!"

"What should we do?" Eddie whimpered, almost crying.

"Let's run!" Quincy suggested.

"My legs won't move," Rob said. We were all paralyzed with fear.

"I think I just peed in my pants," Teddy moaned.

"Me too," said Eddie.

Suddenly an oval hole opened up on the side of the UFO. A disk about the size of a manhole cover slid out like a platform and floated in the air next to the ship.

"Somebody's in there," Quincy whispered.

Then a thing stepped out of the UFO and onto the disk. It was about twelve feet tall. Hairy. Three arms. The disk floated along silently about a foot off the ground. The Bogle twins wrapped themselves around my legs so tightly that I couldn't have moved if I'd wanted to.

"Say something," Rob whispered to me.

"*You* say something."

"You're the CEO."

It turned out that I didn't have to say anything. The creature spoke first.

"Greetings from the planet Bettendorf," it said, in an accent somewhere between English and Spanish.

"Are . . . y-you going to . . . k-kill us?" I stammered.

"No."

I felt myself exhale.

"As long as you cooperate with me."

I inhaled again.

"I have been visiting your planet for many revolutions around the sun," the hairy thing said. "Now I have returned."

With one of its hands, the thing reached into its own stomach—or the place where its stomach would be, anyway—and pulled out a machine about the size of a telephone. We all gasped.

"Wh-what are you going to do with that?" Rob blubbered. "Are you going to perform bizarre medical experiments on us?"

"Don't give it any ideas, dipstick," Quincy muttered.

"No," the alien replied. "I have come here to take something and bring it home with me."

"Anything," I offered. "Take anything. Just don't hurt us."

"Good," the thing said. "I am going to take . . . your picture."

"What?!"

"Why do you want to take a picture of us?" I asked. The answer was a flash of light that shot out of the machine the thing was holding.

"Hey, wait!" Eddie said. "You didn't give us the chance to say cheese!"

"Quiet, gumby!" I said.

"Bettendorfers do not believe there is intelligent life on other planets. But I have proof. I can sell this photo and make millions of zlotys."

I didn't know what zlotys were, but it sounded like money to me. Now he had me interested. I took a step forward.

"How about giving us a million or two?" I asked.

"Zlotys are balls of dust," the thing informed us.

"You use dustballs for *money*?" Rob asked.

"Bettendorf has no atmosphere," the thing explained. "So dust is virtually nonexistent on my planet. That is why it is so valuable."

The Bogle twins looked at each other. They nodded their heads at the same time, and then Teddy picked up his box of dust and handed it to the alien.

"This is a present," he said. "Five years' worth of dust from my mommy's dryer."

"Congratulations," I said. "You'll be the richest one on Bettendorf."

"Thank you," the thing proclaimed. "I must go now."

The disk began to rise.

"Wait!" Rob called. "You could come to the Earth and photograph *anybody*. Why did you choose us?"

The thing stopped.

"I carefully select the earthlings I choose to photograph," it said. "There is only one kind of earthlings I choose."

"What kind of earthlings are they?" Rob asked.

"Earthlings who have been caught making fake UFO photos."

"Why?" I asked, puzzled.

"Because when you tell others about this, nobody will ever believe you."

The disk began to move back toward the spaceship.

"Wait!" Rob called once again. "How about telling us the secret of the universe or something?"

The disk that the thing was standing on was now next to the large oval hole in the spaceship. The thing turned to us once more.

"Inky . . . dinky . . . pinky," it said.

And then it was gone.

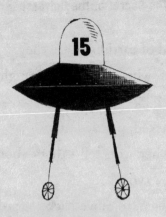

The Future?

We saw it!" we all shouted as we burst, huffing and puffing, into Brian McNight's office at the *Farmington Journal*. "This time we saw it for real!"

"Oh no," he said, slapping his forehead. "Not *you* again."

"Mr. McNight, we swear we saw it!" Rob pleaded.

"Sure, sure. What did you see this time? Bigfoot? The Loch Ness Monster?"

"No, this time we *really* saw a UFO." Rob was practically on his knees.

"I suppose you have more phony pictures too?" Mr.

McNight snorted. "Did you shoot some fake video this time?"

"No, but the alien took a picture of *us*!" I explained.

"And we gave it our collection of dust," added Teddy.

"Get out of here," Mr. McNight said, getting up from his chair. "You kids are annoying. You made a monkey out of me once. It's not gonna happen again."

"It came out of its ship and talked to us!" Rob begged. "You've got to believe us!"

"Yeah, and I suppose it said 'inky dinky pinky,' right?"

"Yes!" we all yelled. "That's the secret of the universe!"

"Did you ever hear the story of the boy who cried wolf?" Mr. McNight said as he led us out of his office. "Well, you're the kids who cried UFO. Now go on home and play with your toys. I've gotten into enough trouble because of you."

Well, so ends the story of the UFO scam. Before we knew it, it was September and time to go back to school. In thinking about it, I guess it wasn't such a boring summer after all. Maybe I didn't get to go to camp. Maybe I didn't make a million dollars (I didn't even make *one* dollar). But I had a blast with Quincy, Rob, Teddy, and Eddie. Plus I got to meet an alien from another planet. How many kids could say that?

Besides, I learned a valuable life lesson—have an extra pack of film with you at all times.

After school let out on the first day, I went outside and climbed up the tree in the field, just for old times' sake. As I sat there thinking about what might have happened if we had pulled off the UFO scam, Quincy and Rob drifted over. Eventually the Bogle twins showed up too. It was almost as if we had been drawn back to the spot where it all started.

"Look at it this way," Rob said as we sat in the tree. "We started out with no money, and we ended up with no money. So in the cosmic scheme of things, it was like none of this ever happened."

I didn't know what he was talking about, but it didn't matter.

"Maybe we could mow some lawns, or wash cars,"

Teddy suggested. "It wouldn't be a lot of money, but a dollar here and a dollar there adds up."

"If we earned a dollar a day, how long would it take us to earn a million dollars?" I wondered.

Quincy pulled a calculator out of her pocket and punched in the numbers.

"Two thousand seven hundred thirty-nine and three quarters years," she said. Everybody groaned.

"We had a brilliant idea that came *so* close to making us millions of dollars," I said. "There are plenty of ideas like that out there. They're just floating around, waiting for somebody to think them up."

"Professional athletes earn millions of dollars," Teddy said. "Maybe we could do that."

"None of us are any good at sports," Eddie told his brother.

"I got it!" I exclaimed, snapping my fingers. "One of us could fall down on the sidewalk in front of a store and sue them!"

"That's even more dishonest than shooting fake UFO pictures," Rob said with a stern look.

"We could get some scratchies,"[1] Quincy suggested.

"Maybe we'd win."

"Fat chance of that ever happening," I scoffed. "You might as well stuff your scratchies up your ears."

"Wait a minute!" Rob exclaimed. "Say that again!"

I looked at him.

"All I said was, 'You might as well stuff your scratchies up your ears.'"

Rob hopped off the branch and paced back and forth on the ground like a tiger. He had that wild, excited, mad-scientist look in his eyes. When we tried to talk to him, he held his hand up for us to wait until he was done thinking.

"I've got it!" he finally shouted, gleefully.

I knew another one of his million-dollar ideas was on its way.

---

[1] "We could get some lottery tickets."

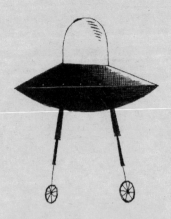

About the Author

Dan Gutman is the author of many books for young people, such as *Honus & Me*, *The Kid Who Ran for President*, *The Million Dollar Shot*, and *Johnny Hangtime*. For more information about Dan and his books, visit his website (www.dangutman.com).